Claire Freedman has written over 50 picture books for children, including many international best-sellers. Claire enjoyed writing this ballerina story and indulging her sparkly pink girly side!

Lorna Brown studied fine art painting at university and works as an artist and illustrator from her cottage in Somerset. Lorna also works as an animal therapist, so she has the perfect balance between art and her love of animals and the outdoors!

This edition published by Parragon in 2013
Parragon
Chartist House
15–17 Trim Street
Bath BA1 1HA, UK
www.parragon.com

Please retain this information for future reference.

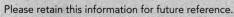

Written by Claire Freedman   Illustrated by Lorna Brown
Edited by Laura Baker   Production by Jonathan Wakeham

ISBN 978-1-4454-9882-9

Printed in China

The Butterfly Ballerina

PaRragon

Bath · New York · Singapore · Hong Kong · Cologne · Delhi
Melbourne · Amsterdam · Johannesburg · Shenzhen

Isabella Ballerina loved ballet.

She liked twirling around
in her pretty leotard.
She loved wearing her
satin ballet shoes.

Best of all, she liked going to Madame Colette's Ballet School. "Come, *mes petites!*" said Madame Colette – who was French and had once been a real ballerina.

"Let us begin by warming up!"

The girls began their bending
and stretching exercises.

"Now, let us practise our ballet positions!" said Madame Colette, clapping her hands, as Miss Robin played a beautiful tune on the piano.

"*Non, non,* Isabella!" cried Madame Colette. "You are pointing the wrong foot again!"

"Oops, sorry!" Isabella said.
"I'm always getting my left
and right muddled up!"

Isabella concentrated very hard, and the
rest of the lesson went really well.
She only turned the wrong way twice!

"*Bien!* Good!" said Madame
Colette. "Wonderful pirouette,
Isabella! Now, I have exciting
news to announce!"

Madame Colette told the girls that they would be putting on their very first ballet show.
"We will dance the Butterfly Ballet!" she said.
"This ballet is set in a beautiful flower garden.

I will choose girls to play raindrop butterflies,

girls to be rainbow butterflies

and one girl to dance the beautiful sunshine butterfly!"

Back home, Isabella told Mummy all about the ballet. "Madame Colette says my ballet is getting better," she said.

"I just wish I could remember my left from my right!"

"This might help my little
Butterfly Ballerina!" Mummy smiled.
She gave Isabella a beautiful
butterfly bracelet.

"Wear it on your right wrist;
then you'll always be able
to tell which way is right,"
Mummy told Isabella.

At each ballet lesson, the girls practised their steps for the Butterfly Ballet.

Isabella kept looking down at her butterfly bracelet to make sure she turned the right way!

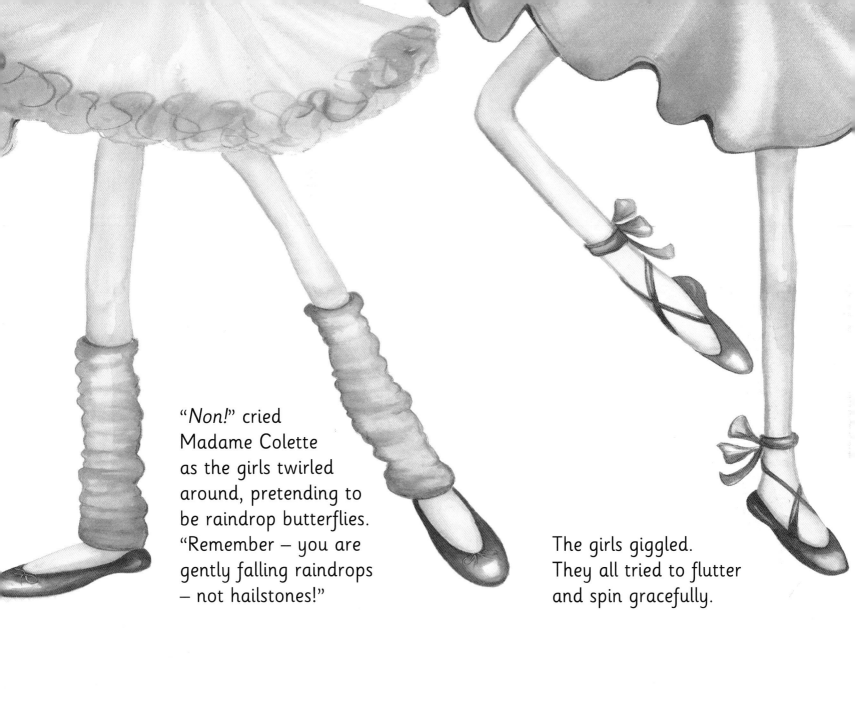

"*Non!*" cried
Madame Colette
as the girls twirled
around, pretending to
be raindrop butterflies.
"Remember – you are
gently falling raindrops
– not hailstones!"

The girls giggled.
They all tried to flutter
and spin gracefully.

Finally the decision time came and Madame Colette told the girls, one by one, if they were going to be a raindrop or rainbow butterfly.

Soon only Isabella was left. "Oh no!" she thought. "I hope Madame Colette isn't leaving me out of the ballet because she's worried I might get my left and right mixed up!"

"Isabella, *ma petite!*" said Madame Colette. "You shall play the sunshine butterfly. As you twirl so beautifully, you will dance the final pirouette!"

Isabella just hoped she would turn the right way!

The week before the show, Isabella
practised her pirouettes everywhere!
She twirled in the garden...

in her
bedroom...

and at the park with
her best friend, Hannah.

On the night of the big show, all the girls dressed in gorgeous tutus and delicate, shimmering butterfly wings. They tied matching ribbons in each other's hair. "Now we feel like real butterflies!" they giggled to each other.

Each girl's family was waiting in the audience. The lights dimmed. Miss Robin began to play the piano and beautiful music filled the room. The ballet was about to begin!

Out danced the raindrop butterflies, flitting gracefully from flower to flower. Their sparkly costumes twinkled in the soft lights.

Next, the colourful rainbow
butterflies danced out,
linking arms before
a beautiful
arching rainbow.

At last it was Isabella's turn to dance. Nervously, she touched her butterfly bracelet.

Then she stepped lightly onto the stage.

She fluttered to the middle, took a deep breath and twirled the most perfect pirouette she had ever twirled!

The girls joined Isabella on stage, and they all
curtsied to the final tinkling notes of the music.
Isabella smiled and touched her beautiful bracelet.

"Oops!" she giggled. She had curtsied with the wrong foot forwards, but it didn't matter one little bit.

She would always be Isabella, Butterfly Ballerina!

Verbs

Verbs are doing words.
They tell us what people are doing.

singing

reading

running

eating

GRAMMAR *Focus*

Write down what each person is doing.
Choose a **verb** from the box to go with each picture.

jumping

writing

playing

swimming

sleeping

drinking

1 _____

2 _____

3 _____

4 _____

5 _____

6 _____